The
Reindeer
Girl

Turn to the back of the book for a
glossary of special words and to find out more
about the world of the Sami

STRIPES PUBLISHING
An imprint of Little Tiger Press
1 The Coda Centre, 189 Munster Road,
London SW6 6AW

This paperback edition first published
in Great Britain in 2013.

Text copyright © Holly Webb, 2013
Illustrations copyright © Artful Doodlers, 2013
Cover illustration copyright © Simon Mendez, 2013
Author photograph copyright © Nigel Bird
Puppy and kitten illustrations copyright © Sophy Williams
My Naughty Little Puppy illustration copyright © Kate Pankhurst
Photographic images courtesy of www.shutterstock.com

ISBN: 978-1-84715-446-0

A CIP catalogue record for this book is available
from the British Library.

Printed and bound in the UK.

2 4 6 8 10 9 7 5 3

The
Reindeer
Girl

HOLLY WEBB

stripes

For Tom, Robin and William

~ HOLLY WEBB

CHAPTER
ONE

Uncle Tomas glanced round at Lotta from the front seat of the car. "I know you really want to see your grandparents, and your great-grandmother. But the thing is, on the way from the airport to their house, we will go past the reindeer farm…"

Lotta gave a little gasp. "Right past it?" she asked, looking pleadingly between her mum and dad.

"Oh, I don't know…" Lotta's mum said, shaking her head doubtfully. "We're a bit tired from the flight. And Mormor and Morfar and Oldeforeldre will be at their house, waiting to see us."

Lotta nodded, trying not to look disappointed. This was her first trip to Norway, and although her grandparents – she called them by their Norwegian names, Mormor and Morfar – had been over to London to visit them several times, she had never met her oldeforeldre. Her great-grandmother was too frail to travel so far, but Lotta loved speaking to her on the phone. One of the reasons that they'd come to Tromsø this year was that Oldeforeldre was going to be ninety, two days before Christmas. They were going to have a special party to celebrate.

But the reindeer... For Lotta, they were one of the most exciting parts of the trip. They were all mixed up in her mind with the deep snow, and the cold, and the amazing Christmasiness of everything. Even Tromsø airport had been full of beautiful Christmas decorations. And as soon as they had stepped outside, she had breathed in the crisp, freezing air and suddenly felt even more excited. Which she hadn't thought was possible.

Ever since she could remember, her mum had told her stories about Oldeforeldre and the reindeer. They were Lotta's favourite bedtime stories. After her mum had read her way through a stack of picture books, Lotta would always ask for one last story – "a real story now, about Erika and the reindeer."

Erika was her great-grandmother. When she was a little girl she had lived in the forest with her family, who were Sami reindeer herders. Some of the time she had slept in a tent that her family packed up in the mornings and carried on a sledge. Erika had ridden on the sledge when she was too tired to walk or ski, as her family travelled with the reindeer on their long journeys across the Finnmark highlands. It was a lot more interesting than living in a normal house and going to school every morning. In her mind, Lotta thought of Erika as the reindeer girl. She was desperate to meet her.

But she was desperate to meet the reindeer, too. There had been two lifesize model ones in the airport, along with a lot of funny elves that Uncle Tomas had told her were called *nisse*. He said they were a special Norwegian thing, and Mormor had lots of little ones decorating the house. They had been sweet, but Lotta just wanted to see a real reindeer. She had read about them and tried to find out more about Oldeforeldre's life as a reindeer herder. But it wasn't the same as meeting a real one.

"Actually, it was Oldeforeldre's idea that we should stop at the farm," Tomas explained. "She said that when she spoke to Lotta on the telephone, she was so excited about the reindeer and asked so many questions. She said that Lotta would understand all the stories she had to tell her much better if she met the reindeer first."

Lotta's mum laughed. "All right then. Between the two of them, I don't think we have much choice. I think Lotta might be more excited about seeing the reindeer than the family."

Lotta went pink. "That isn't true! I'm just excited about both."

"Good. We will stop at the reindeer farm then. None of our family herd reindeer in the same way that Oldeforeldre did, Lotta," Uncle Tomas added. "Your great-uncle Aslak runs the farm, but he feeds the reindeer now. They don't roam wild."

Lotta nodded. "I suppose nobody goes travelling with the reindeer now," she said, a little sadly.

"It's a hard life," Uncle Tomas said, shrugging. "But some families still do. They use snowmobiles mostly, though, not sledges. Ah, we're nearly there. Just this turning here." He turned the four-wheel drive off the main road, up a steep lane and through a set of huge gates. There was a sign on them, but Lotta couldn't understand what it said. Her mum did talk to her in Norwegian and she knew a little bit, but she found it hard to read.

They piled out of the car, and Lotta was glad of her smart new red coat – it had been bought from a sports shop, and it was thick and padded, meant for skiing. Her mum had said that her old coat wouldn't be warm enough for the Norwegian winter. Even so, Lotta shivered a little as she pulled on her knitted mittens. Mormor had sent them to her, when they had first decided to visit for Christmas. Mormor had said there was thick snow already and she would need them. Lotta loved the white snowflake pattern knitted into the red wool.

"Ah, you've come!" A huge bear of a man, with a thick brown beard, was hurrying out of the farmhouse towards them. "Little Lotta!" He hugged her, and he was so big that Lotta's feet lifted off the ground. "My mamma says you are a reindeer girl, too, and I have to show you the reindeer."

His mamma – that was Oldeforeldre, Lotta realized. "Yes, please!" she told him, rather shyly. His English was amazingly good, although a little slow and thickly accented.

He took her hand, her mitten tiny inside his huge, fur-lined glove, and led them over to a shed that was built on to the side of the house. "I have two reindeer in here," he explained. "Both a little lame, so I brought them inside to recover." He opened the wooden door gently and there was a scuffling noise from inside as two reindeer stood up in their stalls.

Lotta took a step back in surprise – somehow she hadn't expected them to be quite so big. But then she smiled delightedly. "Oh, they're beautiful," she murmured. "Can I … can I pat them?"

"Mmmm, these two are quite tame. I have been feeding them while they are in here, so they are used to me. Here." Great-uncle Aslak tipped a handful of brown pellets into Lotta's mittened hand. "Give them these."

The reindeer snorted eagerly as they smelled the food and leaned over the metal fence, snuffling.

Lotta stretched out her hands a little cautiously, but the reindeer were both surprisingly gentle as they gobbled up the pellets. "They really like them!" she told her great-uncle.

"Mmmm, they are greedy, these two," he said, smiling.

"Why doesn't this one have any antlers?" Lotta asked, frowning at the bigger of the two reindeer. He looked a bit strange without them, almost bald. But very cuddly.

Great-uncle Aslak laughed. "He is a boy, Lotta. Their antlers drop off in the winter, did you not know? The ladies, they keep theirs a little longer, until after their calves are born. So they can use them to swipe at the boys, if they are being too greedy and taking all the food. They need lots of food, the mothers, to grow their calves. They are carrying the babies all through the winter. This one here, she will have her baby in April, perhaps."

"Oh! So this is a mother reindeer?"

Lotta asked. The reindeer was nuzzling hopefully at her mittens, as though she thought Lotta might have more food hidden in there somewhere. Her antlers were enormous, Lotta thought, and her nose was soft and velvety. Now she knew the difference, Lotta could see that she was a girl. She was a little smaller, and she didn't have the thick, shaggy white fur round her neck that the deer in the next pen had. She was quite big round the middle, too, although Lotta couldn't really see a bump.

"Yes, Lotta, I should have told you about the antlers," her mum said, reaching over to stroke the reindeer, too. "Whenever you see pictures of Father Christmas with reindeer pulling his sleigh, they're all girls!"

Lotta giggled. "That's silly! Ooooh!" The mother reindeer had got impatient, and gently butted the side of Lotta's head – an obvious demand for more food.

Great-uncle Aslak tutted. "Greedy! Here, give them a little more, Lotta. They will love you forever now."

"I love them, too," Lotta said, looking into the mother reindeer's dark eyes as she delicately gulped down the pellets. "Thank you for letting us see them."

"Ah, you can come back again and I will take you out to see the rest," Great-uncle Aslak promised. "But Oldeforeldre, she wanted you to see them quickly today. A special start to your visit, she said."

Lotta nodded. "It was perfect…"

Lotta stood hesitating in the doorway of Oldeforeldre's room, with her mum and dad behind her. Not only was it the first time she had met her great-grandmother – she was pretty sure it was the first time she had met someone who was almost ninety years old. Oldeforeldre had been born in 1923, really a lifetime ago. The world had been so different then. Oldeforeldre's world especially.

Lotta had always felt like she knew Oldeforeldre Erika, the little girl from Mum's stories. But now she was almost frightened to meet someone who had lived through all that time.

She stared over at the tiny lady sitting in the armchair by the stove and smiled shyly at her.

"Lotta!" Oldeforeldre sat up straighter

and reached out her arms. "You are here!"

Lotta's mum gently pushed her forward, and Lotta walked in. The small room was full of all sorts of things. There were pieces of embroidery hanging on the walls, and shelves with carvings made of reindeer horn. Her mum had some like that at home. There was even a knife with a carved horn handle on one wall. Oldeforeldre lived with Mormor and Morfar, as she found it hard to manage living by herself now. But she had brought her treasures with her from her old house. She slept in here, too, with all her special things. Her bed was in one corner, piled up with brightly coloured blankets.

Her great-grandmother patted the arm of the chair invitingly, and Lotta perched on it, looking down at her. She had white hair, pulled back into a bun, and she was very wrinkled. But her face was quite tanned, not pale as Lotta had imagined it would be.

"You look so ... familiar," Oldeforeldre murmured slowly. Lotta realized she was having to translate her thoughts into English – Mum had warned her that her great-grandmother didn't speak English quite as well as the rest of the family. But her English was still a lot better than Lotta's Norwegian. And Lotta didn't speak any of the Sami languages at all.

"Who do I look like?" she asked curiously.

"My little cousin – she was called Lotta, like you. She was a year younger than me – we travelled together, with the reindeer. Such special times." Oldeforeldre sighed. "She had dark hair like you, too, with the little plaits and the fringe. So pretty." She patted Lotta's cheek. "Kristin, pass me the photograph album. You will remember

24

the photos – I told you these stories, too, so many times." Oldeforeldre smiled at Lotta's mum.

Lotta's mum reached for a battered-looking album covered in green cloth, opened it and passed it to her grandmother. She then sat down on the floor next to them so that she could see the photos, too.

"There! That was taken on our last winter journey before we were sent off to school. Look, do you see the likeness? So much like Lotta…"

Lotta peered at the faded brown-and-white photo. Two girls, both about the same age she was now, in beautiful dresses. They had full skirts, with bands of embroidery all round. Her great-grandmother, Erika, had a cap on. A Four Winds cap, Mum had said it was called, with its four peaks – a little bit like a jester's hat. But the other girl, this other Lotta, was bareheaded, beaming at the camera, with one front tooth missing, just like Lotta had now. There was a dog sitting beside them, with his tongue hanging out a bit, so he looked like he was smiling, too.

"You got sent away to school?" Lotta asked, looking at the two girls in the photo. They looked too young to go away from their family.

"Yes. But we were lucky, Lotta – we went together. We were not so lonely. My poor brother Matti, he knew no one when he first went to school."

"Was it fun?" Lotta had read books about girls at boarding school, always having midnight feasts and adventures. If you didn't mind being away from home, it might be fun, she supposed.

"Sometimes." Oldeforeldre sighed. "But we were not supposed to talk our own language, Lotta. We were there to become Norwegian and not Sami, and Sami was all we knew. It was very hard."

"It sounds horrible!" Lotta exclaimed.

"You can see why this last journey together was so special for us both." Oldeforeldre smiled down at the girls in the photograph.

Very gently, Lotta reached out and stroked one finger over the picture, wishing she could be part of their story, too. She sensed her mum reach out to stop her, but Oldeforeldre gently pushed her back.

"No, Kristin, Lotta can touch. I want her to understand. I remember that journey so clearly..."

CHAPTER
TWO

"Mmmm, I love the gingery smell." Lotta sniffed happily, as Mormor pulled another tray of *pepperkaken* out of the oven. "You've made loads! Are there lots and lots of people coming to this party?"

Mormor nodded. "All the relatives! One of my cousins has brought her family from America, even." She smiled. "Those look beautiful, Lotta."

Lotta's mum laughed. "Too pretty to eat!"

Lotta admired the curls of icing she'd used to decorate the biscuits. Although she might have to be a bit less fancy with the others or she'd never get them all done in time for the party tonight.

"Ah!" Mormor peered out of the window. "There's your father and Tomas!"

"With the Christmas tree?" Lotta squeaked.

When they'd first got to Mormor and Morfar's house two days before, Lotta had been surprised that there was no Christmas tree. She had supposed that they just didn't have them in Norway. It seemed funny, though, because there were spruce trees everywhere and so many Christmas decorations.

But that morning Uncle Tomas had explained that the day before Christmas Eve was called Little Christmas Eve. This was the real beginning of Christmas time in Norway. It was traditional not to put up the tree until then.

Lotta jumped up and ran out into the hall. Dad and Uncle Tomas were struggling inside with the most enormous Christmas tree she had ever seen.

"Backwards?" Dad suggested, trying not to take out the light fitting, and Uncle Tomas nodded, reversing to squeeze through the living-room door.

The tree was so big it only just fitted in the space in the corner of the room. It was beautiful and it had the most amazing piney smell. The scent mixed with the gingery biscuits, and Lotta thought it smelled exactly like Christmas.

"Here are the decorations, look." Morfar hurried in with two large boxes, and Mum and Uncle Tomas started to unpack them, laughing as they recognized the old ones that they remembered from

when they were children.

Lotta stared as they started to clip little metal candle holders on to the branches. Mum and Dad would *never* have had real candles on their Christmas tree at home. Real candles that Uncle Tomas lit! Norwegians were very fond of candles, Lotta decided. She could see why – they were far prettier than fairy lights. Dad didn't look at all sure about them, though.

"Like it?" Uncle Tomas asked, nudging Lotta with his elbow, as he lit the last of the candles.

"It's perfect," Lotta told him seriously. "But I think you could have got a bigger tree," she added, grinning.

Uncle Tomas rolled his eyes, and Dad snorted with laughter. The star they'd put on the top of the tree was actually scraping the ceiling.

"Oh, Lotta, you look beautiful!" Mormor beamed at Lotta as she walked down the stairs. "What a perfect party outfit."

Lotta smiled at her grandmother. The dress was one of her Christmas presents, but Mum and Dad had given it to her early, so that she could wear it to the special party. She had wanted a Norwegian folk costume ever since she had seen pictures of her mum wearing hers – and then she'd found out that her mum still had her *bunad* costume, hanging at the back of her wardrobe!

Lotta's wasn't a real *bunad*, because the real ones were made out of heavy wool, and had gold and silver threads woven into the embroidery. They were really, really expensive. But yesterday Mum had told Lotta that they were going on a shopping trip. She explained to Lotta that she'd arranged for a shop in Tromsø to find some children's folk costumes the right size for her. Then she would be able to wear the Norwegian dress at the party for Oldeforeldre's birthday on Little Christmas Eve.

As she reached the bottom of the stairs, Lotta did a little twirl in the hallway. She had chosen a dress with a black skirt, and a red and gold top a bit like a waistcoat, over a frilly white blouse. It wasn't anything like the party clothes she wore at home, but it felt right to wear it here.

Uncle Tomas and his wife, Lotta's Aunt Caroline, had traditional costumes, too, and so did their tiny baby, Hanna. Mum was wearing her *bunad*, and even Lotta's dad was wearing black trousers, and a shirt with full sleeves and embroidery down the front. Dad had said he'd wear the proper costume if Mum wanted him to, but she could see that he hated the look of the knee breeches and stockings! Lotta thought that Morfar, Uncle Tomas and Great-uncle Aslak looked very smart, though.

Mormor and Morfar's house was full of people, and amazingly noisy. Luckily, Mum had said Lotta could stay up late, since it was a special occasion. There was no way she'd be able to sleep in their room upstairs with this noise going on.

People kept rushing up to them and hugging her mum. Lotta wished she could understand what they were saying better, although she soon worked out what the Norwegian for "and this must be Lotta!" was. After a while she wandered off and perched on the windowsill, admiring everyone's clothes.

"Why don't we go and get something to eat?" her dad suggested, coming to find her. "I bet there's hot chocolate, as well."

Lotta nodded, and they threaded their way through the beautifully dressed crowd, making for the big table, which was piled with food. The *pepperkaken* biscuits that Lotta had decorated with Mum and Mormor were there. She was pretty sure she had seen one of her American cousins eating one.

They hadn't got very far towards the food table when someone stopped Lotta's dad to talk to him. Lotta rolled her eyes and went on without him. She was hungry now, and she could smell the party food.

In the centre of the table were great big plates of *lutefisk*. Lotta wasn't sure about that. It was dried fish, and Mum said it was delicious, but Dad had whispered to her that he thought it was horrible, and he always had to pretend to like it to keep Mormor happy when they visited. Lotta took some of the bits of bacon that went with it, though, and the potatoes. And she loved the roast pork rib, which was already carved in slices. She balanced a couple of biscuits on the edge of her plate, too, and then went to look for somewhere to sit.

The thing was, everywhere was so full of people, all talking louder and louder. Lotta blinked in the candlelight and wished there was somewhere quieter she could go.

"Are you all right, Lotta?"

Lotta turned round slowly, hoping it was someone she knew. Oldeforeldre was standing behind her, leaning on her walking stick. She was smiling, and Lotta beamed back.

"You look lovely in your dress, Lotta. But tired. Shall we go and sit in my room?"

"Oh, please." Lotta nodded. "I've got cookies, look. We can share them." She followed her great-grandmother through the main room, and they both sighed with relief as the door shut behind them and the noise of the party went down to a quiet buzz. It was cosy in the little room, with the wood stove going and the dim light making the horn carvings gleam.

"Happy birthday!" Lotta said excitedly, as she sat down on the floor with her plate in front of her. "Oh, sorry! Maybe I shouldn't make you sit in here when this is your party."

She looked at Oldeforeldre uncertainly, but her great-grandmother sniffed. "It is *my* birthday, Lotta, and *I* want to have a quiet sit down. I have been talking to everyone for hours already, it seems to me."

Lotta nodded. "I know what you mean. Your dress is beautiful – it isn't like anyone else's at all."

Oldeforeldre wasn't wearing a white blouse with a dress over it, like Lotta's.

Instead her dress was a beautiful bright blue wool, with red and gold embroidery round the neck and shoulders, and an embroidered belt, too.

Oldeforeldre nodded and smiled. "Ah! Yes, this is a Sami dress, Lotta. I wear it only for special occasions now, but when I was younger, this is what we wore all the time. Always the dress. And it was made out of reindeer skin then, not cloth."

"Reindeer skin!" Lotta squeaked, horrified. That was awful, like wearing a fur coat.

Oldeforeldre laughed. "But yes, Lotta! You know my family were reindeer herders. We lived with the reindeer all through the year. They gave us everything. Meat. The skins to wear." She pulled the photograph album from the shelf and turned to the photo of herself and her cousin Lotta. "Even our shoes were made of reindeer skin, can you see?" She pointed to the boots the two girls were wearing, with strange, curled toes. To Lotta, they looked like the kind of thing an elf would have. "These days our costumes are made from wool, and sometimes we wore wool dresses back then, too. But reindeer skin is the warmest thing to wear in the snow."

"It still seems cruel..." Lotta murmured, nibbling her biscuit.

"Mmmm. It was a very long time ago, Lotta. Perhaps people feel differently today. But we did not waste anything that came from our reindeer – even the thread we used to sew our coats and boots was made from the reindeer sinews. I remember watching my mother tearing them with her teeth to make the thread."

Lotta shuddered. "So you didn't have a farm, like Great-uncle Aslak's?" she asked, wanting to change the subject.

"No, no! We were herders. We lived in a village in the winter – little huts, built out of wood and turf. See, here." She pointed to another photograph, of a group of round huts. "The reindeer lived in the mountains, until their food began to run out. They had to dig for lichen under the snow – very difficult. Our fathers would go up the mountains through the winter to help them find the best places. Sometimes they would have to move the herd, when the food grew short in one place.

"Then, when the spring came, the mothers would need more food to give them the strength to feed their babies. The men would take them to the calving grounds, and we would follow with the other reindeer. We would take them down to the coast, to the summer pastures, to eat grass instead. We had to help them to get to the pastures on time, before the snows melted and the rivers flooded. So, in the spring, we would be moving and living in tents. *Lavvus* – made of reindeer skin or canvas, on long poles." She pointed to another photo, this time of a family standing outside a big tent that looked a bit like a Native American tipi. "Can you see inside, look? The fire in the middle. Birch branches spread on the floor – and more reindeer skins to sleep on."

"You really *did* make everything out of reindeer skin," Lotta said.

"Mmmm. Those were the old ways." Oldeforeldre sighed. "Now they have snowmobiles. You know? Motor sledges. Not the same as skis and a reindeer sledge."

"You actually had reindeer pulling sledges? Like Father Christmas?" Lotta stared up at her, not sure if she was joking. She hadn't realized anyone really did that.

Oldeforeldre laughed warmly. "Yes. Like Father Christmas. But usually just one reindeer – not lots tied together." She leaned over towards Lotta and whispered, "And not flying, either."

Lotta giggled. "I suppose not. And you and your cousin Lotta went, too?"

"Yes, all the children did. Me, Lotta, my brothers, we all helped. We worked as a family. When the reindeer went to the summer pastures, our fathers and the older cousins took the mother reindeer and the calves, and my mamma and my aunt Inge and us younger ones would take the male reindeer. They could go faster, you see. It wasn't such hard work to look after them."

Lotta nodded, trying to imagine it. Following the herd through the forest, carrying everything they needed on a few reindeer sledges. Camping in a big tent, and curling up round the fire at night. It sounded magical.

Oldeforeldre added more wood to the stove, and the flames crackled and danced. Watching them made Lotta feel sleepy. "Did you have adventures?" she asked, with a little yawn, leaning her head against the arm of Oldeforeldre's chair. "Was it dangerous?"

Oldeforeldre reached down and stroked her hair. "Sometimes. There were eagles, who would try to snatch the little reindeer calves. And wolves in the forests…"

Lotta nodded and yawned again. Real wolves! It sounded like a fairy tale. Two little girls walking through the forest, and a wolf sneaking along behind…

CHAPTER
THREE

L otta woke up, yawning and blinking. She rubbed her cheek against the furry rug she'd been sleeping on, and wriggled away from the shaft of sunlight. She didn't want to get up yet. The party had gone on late, so late that she didn't remember going to bed last night at all.

Actually, she didn't even remember the end of the party. Maybe someone had carried her upstairs? Curious now, Lotta sat up and stretched, looking around to see where she was.

Then she clutched at the furry rug in a panic. This wasn't her grandparents' house in Tromsø. She didn't think it was a house at all. She was sitting on a pile of soft brown furs, by the side of a fire. A real fire, not a stove. It was right in the middle of the floor, surrounded by a few big stones. Cautiously, Lotta reached out to touch one – it was still warm, even though the fire was mostly ashes now.

It was a tent, she decided. A big, cone-shaped tent, with wooden poles. The last smoke from the fire was drifting wispily up and out of a hole at the top, and there was a door folded back. She could see out of the opening – tall, dark trees were rising out of the snow, their branches waving.

The wind was howling, shaking the sides of the tent. She could hear bells ringing, too – not church bells, but smaller ones, clonging and jingling close by, mixed with a heavy, thudding noise, like horses trotting.

"Lotta, are you going to sleep all day? Get up!" A girl a little older than Lotta slipped in through the open door and stood in front of her, hands on her hips. "You're so lazy!" she giggled. "You're worse than Nils and Matti. Come on. My pappa says they're about to leave. And your pappa asked me to find you. You need to come and say goodbye."

Lotta nodded. She didn't understand what was happening, but if she needed to say goodbye to her dad, then of course she would go. Perhaps he could explain what was happening – and where he was going.

She pushed back the furry covers, and ran her hands down the blue cloth of her dress. Then she followed the other girl to the door of the tent, blinking as she came closer to the bright light. Even though the tent was surrounded by snow, the day was glittering and brilliant. Icicles hung from the tree branches, sparkling in the sun.

The snow must be thawing, Lotta thought, frowning to herself. You only got icicles when there were drips that froze again, she was sure. Wasn't it strange for the snow to be melting away at Christmas time? She was sure that Mum had said there would be snow until April, at least.

"Lotta, put your boots on!" the other girl said, popping her head back through the door. "Are you still half asleep?"

Lotta gave a nervous sort of laugh. "I think I must be," she muttered, looking down at the boots, which were waiting by the door. They were full of soft, dried green grass, like sweet hay, and she wondered if the other girl was playing a trick on her. She crouched down to pull the grass out, and then saw that the other girl's boots had grass in, too. She could see it sticking out just a little between the boots and the pretty red embroidered bands that tied around the boots and the furry leggings the girl was wearing. Perhaps the grass was instead of socks? Lotta thought, dazedly. But *why*?

She wriggled her bare feet into the boots, wincing a little as she stuffed her toes in. She'd expected the grass to be itchy and horrible, but it didn't feel too bad, and the boots fitted perfectly.

"Erika! Lotta! Come on!" Someone was calling from outside, and the other girl – was she called Erika then? – grabbed the long bands of woven red ribbon that were piled next to the boots. Lotta blinked as she watched her. Oldeforeldre's name was Erika...

"Oh, hurry up!" Erika started to wind the bands round the tops of Lotta's boots. "I don't want to miss saying goodbye.

We won't see them for weeks once they go off to the calving grounds with the mother reindeer." Erika finished tying the bands, and then grabbed a thick fur jacket and a hat, and slung them at Lotta. "Let's go!" She grabbed Lotta's hand and dragged her out of the tent, running through the snow towards the growing noise outside.

It was reindeer hooves, Lotta now realized. Thudding and thumping on the snow, as the reindeer milled around. The pregnant mothers and last year's young calves had been separated out from the males, who were shut up inside a strange sort of enclosure made out of fabric wrapped round tall poles, like a fence. They were grunting and stamping, and the mothers and young reindeer were skittish and jumpy, as if they knew they were about to set off.

"Lotta! There you are!" A big man was stomping towards them, wrapped in a thick, heavy fur coat that made him almost as wide as he was tall. He wrapped Lotta in a huge hug and lifted her off her feet, swinging her round and making her laugh in delight. It was something her dad did sometimes.

But this wasn't her dad. Lotta stared at the smiling man, as he set her down in the snow. He was taller and bigger, and smelled different. Yet she felt safe with him, somehow. It was as though she'd stepped into his daughter's place – Lotta, the cousin her great-grandmother had told her about. As well as her clothes, and her boots with the grass in…

Lotta stepped back a little, watching this man who felt strangely like her father, and the other men who were bustling around, packing bundles on to sledges and harnessing themselves up to the reindeer. It looked as though the reindeer were actually going to pull some of them along on skis. It was another world…

"Are you all right, Lotta? Have you said goodbye to Pappa?"

"Mamma!" Lotta looked up at her, blinking tearfully – everything felt so strange, and she was frightened. The woman smiling at her had a very faint look of her mother – the way her eyes went when she smiled, perhaps. She wrapped her arms round Lotta and hugged her tightly.

"Oh, Lotta, don't be sad! We'll see Pappa again in a week or two! We'll meet them all at the calving grounds, won't we? Pappa and your uncles."

"It won't be long at all," Pappa said.

Lotta nodded. It must be just before the spring migration, she thought. Oldeforeldre had told her about it. When her father and her uncles took the mother reindeer off to the calving grounds. Then her mother and her aunts and some of the cousins came on afterwards with the males, once the mothers had had their babies in peace. Then they would all travel on to the summer pastures together.

But what was Lotta doing in the middle of all this? Eighty years in the past? Was it a dream? It didn't feel dream-like at all. She could smell the reindeer. A strong, horsey smell, like in the stable at Great-uncle Aslak's farm. She didn't ever remember smells in dreams before.

She had gone to sleep at a party, leaning against her great-grandmother Erika's chair, and listening to the story of her time as a reindeer girl. Lotta had fallen asleep, thinking of snow, and reindeer, and wolves. And she'd woken up *here*.

Inside the story.

CHAPTER
FOUR

L otta's pappa stared down at Lotta and Erika seriously. "I'm leaving you two to look after the mother reindeer and her calf, you understand? It's your special job."

"Yes, Uncle Peter." Erika elbowed Lotta gently, and Lotta gave a little gasp. "We understand, don't we, Lotta? We'll make sure she's all right. And her new calf."

Lotta nodded, gathering her wits. It was as though she had to pull in a fishing net, full of all the things she needed to know. She tried to think of everything Oldeforeldre had told her about her life as a reindeer girl, but there were so many gaps. She'd just have to do her best.

She didn't understand what had happened, but there was no time to think about it. It must be a very strange and real dream, that was all. And now her pappa was asking them to do something important.

"He's still not feeding well from his mother," Pappa said, frowning. "In a week or so you can try and give him a handful of grain every so often. And some for her, too. You have to keep her strength up so she has enough milk for him. He's very small, and he's her first calf. She needs you to help her."

"We will," Lotta whispered, and her pappa leaned down to hug her again, his bristly chin scratching her face and making her laugh.

"I'll miss you. Look after your mamma while I'm away, too, yes?"

Lotta's mamma tugged the flaps on her tall red hat closer around her ears.

"The wind is bitter," she said. "Make sure you build your fire well tonight, Peter. There's some dried fish on one of the sledges, you must eat properly."

"Of course, I will." He wrapped one arm round each of them. "I promise. And I'll see you soon, when we all meet up at the calving grounds."

One of the other men was calling, and he looked round. "Time to go." He walked back over to the big wooden sledge at the front of the line and checked the harness.

"I hope Growler pulls the sledge well, don't you?" Erika said, coming up beside her, and nodding at the reindeer that was going to pull the sledge. "I loved helping your pappa to train him this winter. It was fun, wasn't it?"

Lotta nodded, trying to look as though she knew what Erika meant.

"He doesn't seem worried by the harness, does he? But then we spent ages getting him used to it. Oh, my pappa's calling." She dashed off towards one of the other men, huge and tall in his fur coat, and Lotta was left alone again.

Growler grunted loudly, staring at Lotta, as though he wanted something. She walked over slowly, and hesitantly began to stroke him and rub his soft nose, the way she had with the reindeer at the farm.

They must have named him Growler because of the noises he made, she thought. He was doing it now, making deep, throaty growls as he nuzzled at the pockets of Lotta's heavy fur coat.

He seemed to think there was food in there.

"I don't have any," Lotta told him apologetically. "I'm not quite who you think I am. But I'll try and give you some food next time I see you. You do look so silly with half your antlers gone like that," she added, with a little laugh. Growler had only lost the antlers on one side, which made him look all lopsided and a bit dopey.

She stayed there, patting Growler and stroking his ears, while everyone bustled around. She could feel the little notches cut in the edges of his ears. Mum had told her about those in one of her stories – the marks that showed he belonged to her family.

Her pappa was putting on his wooden skis, tucking the ties carefully under the curly toes of his reindeer-skin boots. *So that's why they have such funny-shaped boots*, Lotta thought. *It helps to hold the skis on…*

She shook her head in confusion. She felt like she was two people at once. The Lotta who should really be here, who knew all these people rushing around her and obviously loved Growler. And the other Lotta, who had no idea what was going on and was just fumbling her way through the story, trying not to let everyone see that she shouldn't really be there.

Growler nudged her lovingly, and she leaned against his warm side for a moment with a soft sigh. *He* didn't seem to think that she was the wrong Lotta.

What was she doing here? Lotta wondered. She had never had a dream like this before. One that was so real, and full of things she was sure she didn't know enough about to dream. The amazing clothes that everyone was wearing. The thick blue cloth tunics – Oldeforeldre had said they were called *gákti*, and that the heavy fur jacket was a *beaska*.

Lotta blinked, realizing that she must be speaking the same language as everyone

else, as well. It was as if she had just
slipped back in time to the world her great-
grandmother had described. Oldeforeldre
had shown her photographs and told her
stories, but Lotta hadn't really been able
to imagine what her great-grandmother's
Sami life was like.

And yet here, in this dream, somehow
she could see it all so clearly.

So perhaps it wasn't a dream after all?
Perhaps it was something more...

Lotta stood watching as the reindeer
herd set off. Her father's dog, a beautiful
creature with a golden-orange coat, leaped
down off the sledge where he'd been sitting
and began to howl. Pappa was telling him
to, Lotta could see now. He must have

been trained to howl on command, to
keep the reindeer bunched together. It
made sense. If they straggled out in a long
line, it would be harder to make sure they
were all keeping up. There were other
dogs hurrying round the herd, too – each
of her uncles and cousins seemed to have
their own herding dog.

She could hardly see the herd now. The final few reindeer were vanishing over the rise in the snowy ground, and one of her uncles was turning back to wave one last time, before following on his skis. All that was left was the churned-up snow, marked by hundreds of hoofprints and the sledge runners.

"Come on, Lotta. Let's go and check on that little calf." Erika grabbed her hand and pulled her away. "Aunt Inge, we're going to see the new baby reindeer!" she called to Lotta's mamma.

Lotta followed Erika past the *lavvus* to a quiet space among the scrubby trees where a reindeer was grazing, digging through the snow with her front hoof and looking for lichen. She kept glancing around restlessly, but when the two girls

came close, she backed away, towards
a small brown bundle curled up in the
snow.

"Isn't he tiny?" Lotta whispered. The
calf was so small and soft-looking, its fur a
golden brown, darker round his nose and
his eyes, almost as though he was wearing
sunglasses. She longed to stroke him,
or pick him up, but she didn't think his
mother would like it.

"Well, he is only a couple of days old," Erika pointed out. "I wonder why he came so early. It's nice to see one so young – because we stay here and the mothers go off to the calving grounds, we hardly ever see such a baby."

"I don't think she wants us to go near him," Lotta said anxiously. The mother reindeer was eyeing them, as though she wasn't sure who to trust. "It must be strange for her, being left behind when all the others have gone to the calving grounds. She probably doesn't understand what's happening."

"I've got some grain for her. If we give her some food, she might let us get closer to the calf." Erika dug into her coat pocket and the reindeer snuffled eagerly, stepping towards the girls.

"She's really hungry." Lotta peered round the reindeer to look at the calf, and he looked back at her shyly, his eyes huge and dark.

Erika laughed as the mother reindeer gobbled eagerly at the grain, and then snuffled against her affectionately. "Do you like us now, hmmm?"

The reindeer calf struggled up on to his long, fragile-looking legs and stumbled over to his mother. He tried to suckle, nuzzling at the fur underneath her, and she peered down at him worriedly.

"Pappa said he wasn't suckling very well," Lotta remembered. "Maybe she isn't making enough milk for him."

Erika nodded. "Well, she should be in the calving grounds, shouldn't she, where the food's better."

The part of the forest they were in now was quite open, without too many trees, and that meant the snow was thick and heavily frozen. Lotta frowned, trying to remember what Oldeforeldre had told her about the reindeer migration. In a week or so, the rest of the herd would follow the mother reindeer to the calving grounds, where the snow would be melting and the grasses showing through. Then, a little later, when all the calves were big enough to make the journey, the two herds would go on together to the summer pastures.

"There isn't a lot of grain to spare for feeding her," Erika murmured. "We have to trade for it, with reindeer hides and dried meat. Grain's expensive." She chewed her lip and dug at the snow with her boot. "She really ought to be feeding herself, but the ice crust over the snow's so hard here. It's taking her ages to dig through it to find the lichen to eat."

Lotta picked up a piece of branch and dug under the snow. It was frozen solid, and she had to work at it. But the reindeer sniffed interestedly as Lotta scraped back the snow, revealing the lichen on the ground. She took a couple of steps forward and began to nibble at it gratefully. Her calf stumbled after her and went on trying to suckle.

"Maybe we could keep helping her dig?" Lotta suggested to Erika, rather uncertainly. Perhaps it was something they weren't supposed to do. She didn't know, after all.

But Erika nodded. "Uncle Peter did say to look after her. That must be the best way to help her, I think." She fetched another branch, and began to scratch in the deep snow. "Ah, look, here you are! A big clump!"

The reindeer pushed Erika out of the way eagerly as she smelled the feathery, greyish-green lichen clump buried in the snow, and both girls giggled.

"We should name them," Lotta said, as she went on digging. "Her and the calf."

Erika looked rather surprised. "I suppose we could. What shall we call her?" She grinned. "Pushy? Greedyguts?"

"No! Something nice." Lotta looked thoughtfully at the reindeer, trying to think of a good name. She still had her antlers, and her coat was beautifully thick. The reindeer stared sideways at Lotta, watching her with one dark eye while she munched on the lichen.

"She's got a mark on her side, here, look." Lotta pointed to a darker patch of fur. "It's almost like a flower. If we call her Flower, then we'll remember, and we'll always be able to pick her out, even when she's back with the others."

She gave a little gulp then, wondering if

she would still be with Erika and Flower when they got to the summer pastures. That was weeks away. Would she be back home by then, with her real family?

With Flower nuzzling against her gratefully as she gobbled the lichen, and the baby reindeer giving her shy looks as he suckled, Lotta wasn't sure if she wanted to go back. Not just yet. She had loved the stories about the reindeer girl so much, and now it seemed she was living them.

And she liked her matter-of-fact cousin, too. Erika seemed to have a silly sense of humour, even though she was a bit bossy. She definitely had a cheeky grin.

"Flower." Erika nodded. "I like it! What shall we call the baby?"

"I don't know." Lotta shook her head.

"He hasn't got any marks. He's just really sweet. We could call him Sweetie, maybe."

"I'm not calling him Sweetie!" Erika snorted. "Imagine shouting that out in front of everybody! My brothers would laugh their heads off. Besides, what about when he's nearly as tall as you? We won't want to call him Sweetie then."

"All right. What's your favourite name?" Lotta said. "Lars? Johan?"

"He doesn't look like a Lars... And Johan would be too confusing, with Cousin Johan as well." Erika stared at the little calf thoughtfully. "He does look like a Karl, though! Let's call him Karl!"

CHAPTER FIVE

L otta and Erika spent the next few days digging up lichen for Flower in between their other chores. Lotta hadn't understood how much hard work being a reindeer herder meant. They had to help their mothers and cousins round up the reindeer every morning, for a start. The reindeer wandered away looking for food during the night, and finding them took a lot of work, made even harder by the intense cold and the biting wind. Lotta was grateful for her reindeer-skin coat, and the furry leggings and boots. She had hated the idea of wearing reindeer skin when Oldeforeldre had told her about it, but now she saw why it was needed. The coat was a lot warmer than the smart red one she had back in her own time.

Lotta and Erika managed to get

Erika's brothers, Matti and Nils, to help with digging for Flower, too. Erika had cunningly told them that there was no way the boys could find as much lichen as the girls could. It was another thing that was strange for Lotta – with no brothers and sisters, she wasn't used to having other children around all the time. She loved it, especially the way she and Erika got to gang up against the boys.

After a week of helping Flower out with her food, the reindeer was starting to look a little bit plumper, and she seemed to be making enough milk to feed Karl properly. Lotta and Erika felt sure she was managing well enough for them to join the boys for an afternoon of ice-fishing on the frozen lake close to the camp.

At home, Lotta wasn't that keen on

fish, but all the food her mamma and Erika's mother, Aunt Astri, cooked over the open fire seemed delicious. Perhaps it was just that she was hungrier. Lotta had never drunk coffee at home, either, but here everyone drank it to warm themselves up.

If they could catch some trout or char, her mamma would cook it for dinner that night, with some dried herbs, perhaps. There were potatoes, too. It would make a delicious change from dried reindeer meat and stew.

"Are you two actually coming?" Matti, Erika's older brother, who was fourteen, stomped past. He was carrying a couple of rods and a long ice-chisel to break through the frozen lake surface.

"We were busy with Flower and Karl!"

Erika told him indignantly. "It isn't as if you've been doing anything useful!"

"Wait for me!" Nils yelled, running after them. He was only seven, the youngest in the big family group, and he hated to be left behind.

"You're only coming if you promise to be quiet," Erika told him sternly, and Nils puckered up his face as if he was about to howl that it wasn't fair.

"Shall we go and get the reindeer skins out of the *lavvu*?" Lotta said quickly, trying to break up the squabble before it started. They would need the skins to sit on while they waited next to the holes in the ice, hoping that the fish would bite. She hooked her arm through Erika's, and hurried her away.

"Sometimes I just want to trip him up

so he falls in a snowdrift," Erika muttered, as she marched back to meet the boys, her arms full.

"He's only little—" Lotta started to say, but Erika glared at her.

"Don't say that! *Everyone* says that! I wasn't annoying when I was little! You just don't understand."

"Mmmm…" Lotta shrugged. She'd had this argument with her friend Grace back home, too. Grace always said that Lotta was lucky being an only child, and she had no idea how horrible brothers and sisters could be. Which was true.

Lotta suddenly felt tears rising up inside her throat. She hadn't thought much about home over the last week – they had been so busy. But however lovely her family here was, she missed home and her friends, and suddenly she had such a clear picture in her mind of her mum and dad. She missed talking with her mum while she cooked dinner, and Dad helping with her homework. She'd never stayed away from them for so long.

"What's the matter?" Erika leaned over to peer at Lotta over the pile of reindeer skins she was carrying. "You're crying! Lotta, what is it? I'm sorry, I didn't mean to snap at you."

"You didn't," Lotta sniffed. "It's all right." She couldn't explain, of course.

"Come on. Let's go and boss the boys about. That'll make you feel better." Erika led her back to where Matti and Nils were waiting with Matti's dog, Cam, and they trudged through the trees towards the frozen lake.

This was the first time that Lotta had
been fishing, here or back at home. She
looked doubtfully at Matti and Erika, as
they stopped in the middle of a wide sheet
of snow and Erika began to spread out the
reindeer skins. It didn't look like a lake to
her. How did they know it was even water
under there?

But Matti was getting out the chisel
and carefully taking the cover off the
blade, ready to chip away at the ice. Nils
and Erika were scooping away the snow,
and Lotta crouched down to help.

The ice was very thick, and it took
Matti a while to break a hole through,
even with the sharp blade of the chisel.
The girls sat and watched, while Nils
danced around, trying to lasso a snow-
reindeer he'd made.

"Are you all right now?" Erika asked Lotta quietly, and she nodded.

"Yes, I was just..." She didn't know what to say. How could she explain?

"You've been so quiet this week," her cousin added, leaning close and looking worriedly at her. "Are you really all right?"

Lotta swallowed, not sure what to say. Of course Erika would have noticed something different about her. She tried to shrug. "I was just a bit sad. Missing Pappa, you know… Oh! What's that?"

A great shape was swooping low over the frozen lake, sending a shadow swirling past them. Lotta flinched and peered up into the sky as a huge, rusty-brown bird swept past. Cam barked loudly and raced back to Matti's side.

"An eagle!" Matti cried, dropping the ice-chisel. "It was huge! Did you see?"

Lotta nodded, still shivering. She knew there were predators out here – wolves and even bears, but she hadn't seen any. The eagle's hooked claws and sharp beak looked terrifying. "Its wings – they seemed to go on forever."

"It was a big one," Erika agreed. "The wings were as wide as Pappa is tall, I reckon. Maybe even wider."

Lotta nodded. Erika's father was one of the tallest people she'd ever seen. "Can we go back?" she asked Erika. "I know we haven't caught anything yet, but I want to check on Flower and Karl…"

Erika looked up at her. "I don't think it would come in between the trees," she said, her voice gentle. "I know they do take calves, but out on the open tundra. Where they can swoop in."

"It was probably coming to see if we'd caught anything," Matti told Lotta. He was through the ice now, and lowering in a baited line. "Maybe it was going to steal our fish."

"I know. But still… I think I'll go back. You stay."

Erika nodded. "Are you sure?"

"Mm-hm." Lotta nodded. "I'll check on Flower and Karl, and then go and fetch some firewood. So we can cook all the fish you catch."

She hurried away towards the line of thin trees round the banks of the frozen lake. Beyond them she could see the two *lavvus*, and the edge of the spruce forest.

Lotta had expected Flower and Karl to be where the girls had left them, but as she reached the spot where she'd last seen them grazing between the trees, she couldn't see them anywhere. "Flower!" she called, running through the trees. "Karl!"

She heard an answering, frightened whinny, and turned to see Flower standing in a small clearing, with Karl beside her. Flower was pawing the ground anxiously as Lotta ran through the trees towards them, and Lotta was sure that the reindeer had seen the eagle, too. Flower glared suspiciously at Lotta for a moment, and then seemed to realize who she was.

Karl bounced up and skittered over to Lotta, coming to nuzzle at her hands. He didn't understand the danger, Lotta thought. "Come on," she said, slapping Flower on the shoulder. "Come on, away from here, back in the trees."

Flower followed her readily, and Karl danced beside them until they were safely in amongst the trees. As she looked back out towards the clearing, Lotta saw the dark shadow of the eagle float over the snow again. She shuddered. Karl would have been small enough for the eagle to carry away in its talons.

Karl nuzzled lovingly at her, and Lotta crouched down to stroke him. Running her mittens over his soft back, the strange, sad feeling she'd had ever since they set off for the lake melted away. He had never come running to her before, she realized, he'd always been too shy.

Flower snorted softly and went back to feeding, and Karl rested his soft chin on Lotta's knees. She was sure that the happy little grunts and sighs he was making as she rubbed his ears and the tiny stubs of his antlers were just like a cat purring.

"You're so handsome, aren't you?" she murmured. "I came running back like that because there was a great big eagle flapping about. I was worried about you." She shivered. "I should think he'll head over towards the calving grounds instead.

There's probably lots more little ones born by now, even littler than you! But Pappa and the others will drive him away. He won't get them. We'll be setting off after them soon, I expect." She smiled at him. "Maybe that's why I'm here. To look after you and get you safely to the summer pastures. You'll love it there. Delicious grass to eat all the time."

She would love to see it for herself. Erika had talked about the glittering waterfalls, and the streams where they could lie watching the fish in the clear water. The summer pastures where the family's herd always went were on an island, not far out from the coast. Close enough for the reindeer to swim to. "You'll be a lot bigger by then," she added, rather doubtfully. Karl still looked awfully small to swim for nearly an hour, even if he would be with hundreds and hundreds of his relatives. But the final migration wouldn't start until all the calves were several weeks old, and by then they would be almost as big as their parents.

"Big enough to look after yourself," Lotta told him, her voice a little sad.

"Come and sit by me." Erika patted the space next to her by the fire.

Lotta squashed herself in. She had been helping her mamma to serve the fish the others had caught that afternoon, and her mouth was watering.

"You did well to get so many," Lotta told her cousin.

"Mm-hm. Matti made three holes in

the end. Even Nils caught two char. But
you were right to go and check on Karl and
Flower," she added. "That eagle could
have tried to come down in the clearing.
I didn't think they'd move."

Lotta nodded, her mouth too full to talk. She was starving. She'd spent a couple of hours hunting for firewood among the trees, staying close to Flower and Karl all the time, and then she'd helped to prepare the meal.

When she'd finished the fish, she took a piece of the flatbread that they had baked over the hot stones round the fire and wiped the buttery juices off her tin plate. Then she sighed happily, looking round at her mamma and her aunts, and her cousins squabbling over the last bits of bread. She was warm and full. And she was with her family – maybe not the family she was used to, but she did belong. She knew she did.

Lotta leaned against Erika's shoulder and smiled as one of her older cousins began to sing a *joik*, staring into the fire and slapping his hand against his leg for a beat. He was *joiking* the reindeer, singing about how they were his life and gave him everything that he needed. As the song rose and fell, Lotta nodded along, smiling, and thinking of Karl and Flower, and how she would do anything to protect them.

CHAPTER
SIX

"Today? Really?" Lotta stared at her mamma in surprise. She hadn't expected them to follow the mother reindeer to the calving grounds for a few more days, but her mother had woken her early, saying that they needed to take down the two *lavvus* and pack up. Her aunt was bustling around already, gathering up the cooking pots as she told Erika and Matti and Nils to hurry.

"Yes. The rivers are starting to melt. If we don't go soon, we'll have to go a much longer way round. The reindeer can swim the rivers, but it's harder for us to cross them. Better to go now, while they're still frozen and we can follow the route we always take. Johan thinks that the stream that feeds the lake is melting. And you've seen the snow falling off the trees."

Lotta nodded. Quite a lot of it had fallen on her, while she was gathering wood the day before. "Do you think Karl will be all right?" she asked. "He's still very little."

Her mamma smiled. "I'm sure he will. I know you think he's tiny, but he's much bigger than he was – you girls have looked after him so well." She gave Lotta a piece of dried reindeer meat to eat, and hurried out to help the older boys gathering in the herd.

Lotta looked around the *lavvu*. It felt like home now – it was hard to imagine that in a little while it would be gone, and all that would be left behind were the marks of the reindeer and a patch of bare ground where the tents had been set up.

She pulled on her boots and coat, and went out to see Flower and Karl. This morning they were close to the *lavvus*, looking around wonderingly as Lotta's mamma and the older boys drove the male reindeer down through the trees, corralling them ready to set off.

"It's all right," Lotta told Karl, who was shifting about skittishly. "You'll like it where we're going. Erika told me it's

not that hard a journey. Through the forest, and along the path of the frozen river for a way. It'll take about four days for us to reach the calving grounds. Then you'll get to meet the other reindeer calves. You'll like that, won't you?"

She led the two reindeer closer into the rest of the herd, petting and soothing Flower, in case she was startled and decided to run off.

All around her everyone was packing up, tying their tools and pots in bundles on the big wooden sledges. Johan and Matti, her two oldest and tallest cousins, were taking down the *lavvus*, folding up the cloth coverings and gathering the long poles. They had more sets of poles waiting at the calving grounds and the summer pastures.

Erika came over, carrying Lotta's long wooden skis with her own, and the girls began to strap them on, ready to set off on the hard day's trek through the forest. They joined up with the column of sledges and waved to Nils, tucked up on a sledge and looking sulky. He was too young to ski for long, Aunt Astri thought, and they needed to move fast today.

Johan set off at the front of the herd, leading his draught reindeer harnessed up to a sledge. Four more reindeer and sledges were harnessed up behind him, each tied to the one in front. And then behind came the milling, stomping mass of the remaining herd.

"I can hardly hear myself think," Erika muttered. Several of the reindeer had bells, and the animals were clanging and grunting and stamping about, while the cousins tried to shoo them in the right direction after the sledges. The dogs darted back and forth, helping to keep the reindeer together. It was very noisy and confusing, and Karl was pressed up against Lotta's legs, watching with wide, dark eyes.

At last, the column set out through the trees, and Karl and Flower and the girls joined on at the end, striding along on

THE REINDEER GIRL

their skis. Karl trotted along quite happily, following his mother.

They trekked on through the woods, noticing the snowmelt dripping from the branches. The thaw was definitely starting to set in. By midday, Lotta's eyes were aching from the glare of the bright sun shining through the trees and sparkling on the snow. Her legs were aching, too, and her skis felt heavy. She wasn't as used to walking on them as the others, of course.

The column of reindeer had been slowly stretching out, as the animals found their own pace, and the leaders seemed a long way away.

"I hope we stop for a rest soon," Erika said, panting a little.

Lotta nodded. "Mmm. My legs hurt. And Karl looks really tired."

The tiny reindeer looked up as he heard his name and let out a mournful honking noise.

"I think he needs to rest, too." Lotta peered up towards the front of the column, trying to see her mamma, or Johan or Matti. "Oh, look, they're stopping!"

"At last..." Erika sighed.

"I think I'll take Karl up to the front and see if there's space for him on one of the sledges," Lotta suggested. "He can't walk much further."

Flower was nosing at Karl, who had sunk down into the snow. Lotta scooped him up in her arms. He was heavy – a full armful now, nearly as big as one of the dogs. She struggled on through the snow, carrying him, with Flower and Erika following wearily behind.

"Are you all right, Lotta?" her mamma called, as she saw her coming. "We're just stopping for a rest and some food."

"Can we put Karl on a sledge?" Lotta asked hopefully. "He's worn out."

Her mamma leaned down to look at the calf, who wriggled anxiously when he saw a stranger coming near. But he didn't have the strength to struggle out of Lotta's arms, even though she could tell he wanted to.

"Yes, we better had, poor little scrap."

Mamma handed out some dried fish, which Lotta ate eagerly. Then Matti came over. He was holding a piece of canvas. "Wrap Karl in this, and then I can tie him on," he suggested, holding the canvas out so that Lotta could swathe Karl's legs in it. Together, they tied him firmly on to the sledge, so that he wouldn't try to leap off when it started moving.

"Why don't you two girls take it in turns to ride with him?" her mamma suggested. "He'll be happier if you're there holding him."

Lotta nodded. "You can go first," she told Erika. She was feeling a lot better now that they'd stopped for a while, and she knew she would be tired later. Erika gratefully took off her skis, and snuggled up on the sledge with Karl. He still looked wary, but he stopped wriggling when he saw that Erika was with him. Lotta strode alongside them on her skis once the herd set off again, and Flower followed behind the sledge, occasionally nosing at the funny little package that was Karl.

In the middle of the afternoon they

stopped to rest again, and this time
Lotta took the place on the sledge. Erika
wrapped a warm reindeer fur around her,
and Lotta huddled up – she was so sleepy,
now that she wasn't walking.

By the time she woke it was dark, and she could see a warmly lit *lavvu* not far away. Her mamma was standing beside her, laughing. "I thought we should probably wake you, Lotta, or you'd sleep the night through on that sledge, you and the little reindeer. Come on." She unwrapped Lotta and helped her to stand up. Lotta yawned and groaned as she stretched her cramped legs, and then crouched down to untie Karl.

"I wonder where your mother is," she said, looking around for Flower. "Mamma, have you seen her?"

Mamma frowned. "No… Not since we stopped here. Erika! Johan! Have you seen the mother reindeer?"

Erika appeared at the door to the *lavvu*, looking worried. "Isn't she here? She was following the sledge!"

"But she always stays close to Karl," Lotta murmured. "Where can she have gone?"

Erika looked upset. "I'm sorry – I was so tired, I was concentrating on walking. I just thought she was there…"

"And I was asleep," Lotta said guiltily. "I don't know when I last saw her – soon after we set off again this afternoon, I suppose."

"The mother? I thought she was at the back of the column," Johan said. "I saw her there earlier on this afternoon."

"She must have got tired and fallen behind!" Lotta cried. "We have to go and find her."

"In the dark?" Johan frowned. "We can't, Lotta. It isn't safe. We have to stay with the herd."

"I know," Lotta said. "But Flower should be with the herd, too, and we left her behind. It's my fault for falling asleep. I was supposed to watch out for her. Please, can't we go back and look?"

Erika nodded. "She might only be a little way back along the trail."

"I'm sorry, girls." Lotta's mamma exchanged glances with Johan and shook her head.

"Tomorrow morning then?" Lotta pleaded.

"I don't think we can wait," her mamma said gently. "She could have wandered a long way off our trail, and we need to keep going, as fast as we can."

"So we just have to leave her?" Erika whispered.

Lotta swallowed back tears. She hated

to think of Flower, lost and all alone without her herd. But then as Karl wriggled in her arms and let out the honking noise that meant he was hungry, Lotta realized something even worse.

Without his mother to feed him, Karl was going to starve.

CHAPTER
SEVEN

L otta lay warmly wrapped up in the *lavvu*, watching the dying embers of the fire. She knew she ought to go back to sleep – it would be another long day tomorrow. But she just couldn't. She had slept a little earlier in the night, worn out from crying, but then she'd woken again.

Flower was out there somewhere. And Karl was tied up to one of the trees, just outside the *lavvu*, hungry and miserable. She and Erika had tried to get him to take some grain, but he'd hardly had any of it. He wanted to feed from his mother, like he always did. And he didn't understand where she had gone.

If they had been with the rest of the female reindeer, Lotta and Erika could have tried to milk one of them and fed the milk to Karl. But here they had no milk to give him at all. And it would take them at least three more days to reach the calving grounds. Karl wouldn't last that long without food.

Lotta sniffed and turned over, listening to the snuffles and soft sighs as the rest of her family slept. Then she heard a plaintive honking noise, and her breath caught in a sob. That was Karl, outside, calling hungrily for his mother.

It was no good. She couldn't leave him out there like this. Even if he did make it to the calving grounds, it would be hard to find a mother reindeer who would feed him as well as her own calf, and they would all be skittish and hard to milk now they had their new babies.

Lotta couldn't let him fade away.

Her pappa had told her to look after Flower and Karl. She couldn't let them all down. She got up carefully, climbing over Erika and Nils and her aunt, and making for the door. The dogs were sleeping, too, and although Cam opened one eye to look at her, Lotta put her finger to her lips, and he didn't bark.

Lotta shrugged on her big coat and her boots, binding them up with practised speed. She smiled wryly to herself, thinking how different this was from eight days ago, when she hadn't even known how to put them on. Then she unlaced the door of the *lavvu*, stepping out into the night cold.

Karl was a pale little shape in the darkness, and he whimpered and groaned as he heard her coming.

"I know," Lotta whispered. "It's all right. We're going to look for her. I know they said we mustn't, but you'll die if we don't find her." She wrapped her arms around the little calf's neck. "I think this might be why I'm here. I've got to find your mother and rescue you both."

She started to untie the woven reindeer-leather rope that was fastening him to the tree, and then thought for a minute. She needed some supplies. They might be away for a good few hours, and she would need food. It seemed unfair, when Karl would be starving, but she would be no good to him if she couldn't keep going, and in this cold, food was necessary. And perhaps she had better bring a knife, just in case. Johan had told her that he had seen bears in these woods, and she remembered Oldeforeldre talking about wolves.

She crept back into the *lavvu*, looking for a knife to borrow. She was searching around by the cooking pots at the edge of the fire, when a hand closed round her foot. Lotta strangled a scream, stuffing her hand into her mouth.

"What are you doing?" Erika whispered. "Why are you up?"

"I'm going to find Flower," Lotta whispered back. "I can't let Karl starve."

"You can't!" Erika hissed. "Not on your own!"

Lotta shook her head stubbornly. "I'm going to. I'm not going to abandon them."

Erika sat up. "I'm coming with you then. I want to find her, too."

Lotta nodded. "All right. Get some food, can you? I'm just finding a knife."

"Bring one for me. And I'd better give the dogs something," Erika added. "Otherwise they might follow us." She laid a little dried meat in front of the four dogs and whispered, "Shhh..."

The two girls crept out, put on their skis and untied Karl.

"We might have to carry him some of the way," Lotta said, as they set off through the trees. "But I want to get him and Flower back together as soon as we can. We can't leave him at the camp."

It was lucky that both girls had slept

in the daytime. Lotta felt wide awake now that they had decided on a plan. The moon was full and bright, and she could quite easily see the tracks of the hundreds of reindeer in the snow, with the marks of the sledge runners and skis here and there.

"We can't miss our way," she said to Erika, smiling with relief. "It's so clear."

Erika nodded. "I know – and the sun is rising earlier and earlier now it's springtime. It shouldn't be more than two or three hours that we're walking in the dark. We might even end up going faster than all of us together were earlier on, you know. The snow's harder in the cold of the night, and we haven't got to keep stopping to chase back any stragglers."

The girls strode out strongly, and even Karl seemed glad to be walking, as though he knew they were going back to find his mother. Lotta had brought a little grain for him, but she was hoping that they'd find Flower soon so that they wouldn't need it.

It was just as the sun was rising, and the light was creeping through the trees, that they came to the frozen river. Erika was sure they had crossed it late in the afternoon of the previous day, when Lotta had been asleep.

"It *is* melting," Erika said, a little anxiously. "I can hear it, the water flowing just under the ice crust."

"Is it safe to cross?" Lotta asked, testing it with her ski.

"I think it is for now. But maybe not for much longer." Erika set out quickly over the ice, and Lotta followed, trying not to hear the creaks and cracking noises as she and Karl crossed the river.

As Lotta looked back, she could see the bright sun shining on the river ice. Erika was right. They didn't have long before it melted.

They hurried on, trying to go faster now, taking it in turns to carry Karl, who was getting wobbly on his legs. Every few minutes they stopped for a rest, and to call out for Flower. Karl joined in, honking his sad, hungry cries.

They had been going for about another hour when Lotta stopped to call out again. "Flower! Where are you? Flower!" She'd grown so used to shouting that she almost went on without really listening for an answer. But suddenly she felt Karl wriggle in her arms.

"What is it? Do you want to get down?"

Karl wriggled again, snorting and honking, and Lotta gasped. He had heard something, she was sure of it.

"Is he all right?" Erika asked, but Lotta shushed her.

"Listen!"

And there it was – only a little way off the beaten trail of hoofprints, in amongst the trees. A loud, sharp whinnying sound. They had found her.

CHAPTER EIGHT

"Flower!" Lotta cried, putting Karl down and pulling off her skis so she could hurry through the trees without tangling them up. "You're here!"

"She's not hurt is she?" Erika gasped, following her into the trees.

"I don't think so." Lotta stroked Flower's nose, smiling as the reindeer snuffled at her fingers. "Oh, but she's stuck. Poor Flower, how did you manage that? Were you hungry? Did you go looking for that nice lichen on the trees?"

Flower had worked her way into a clump of trees and somehow managed to get her thick winter coat wrapped up in the spiny branches of a young sapling. She was completely tangled.

"She must have seen all that lichen and wandered off for a snack," Erika said, trying to pull the twigs out of Flower's fur. "Then she got herself all caught up, and couldn't follow us."

"I'm so glad we found her," Lotta murmured, yanking at the branches. "There! Come on, Flower! Pull!"

The two girls backed away, coaxing Flower to follow them. At first, the reindeer didn't seem to realize that she was free. She shook herself suspiciously, antlers swaying, and then looked down in surprise. All at once she understood that she could move and she gave a great leap, bursting out into the open. She stood there in the snow, her sides heaving and her eyes wild. But then she saw Karl, and she nuzzled at him delightedly.

The little reindeer allowed himself to be sniffed and licked all over, and then he ducked determinedly underneath his mother and started to feed.

Lotta watched him, smiling to herself, and then she hugged Erika. "We did it! Look at them, they're both safe."

Erika nodded. "I know. And it is wonderful. But we have to get back, Lotta." She was looking along the trail, a serious expression on her face, nothing like her usual teasing grin.

Lotta swallowed. She had forgotten. "The river?"

"Mmmm. I'm worried that if we leave it much longer, we won't be able to cross back over. And then we'll lose the trail."

Lotta glanced down at Karl, who was still feeding. He didn't look as though he wanted to stop any time soon. "He's so hungry..." she said. "We can't make him go on just yet."

But Flower was sniffing at the air, turning her head from side to side. She looked as worried as the girls, and then she turned and began to nose gently at Karl, pushing him away.

He honked crossly and tried to keep feeding, but Flower began to walk off down the trail, and he stumbled after her.

"She knows!" Lotta stared at Flower. "Did you see that? She knows we need to keep going!"

"Maybe she can smell the river?" Erika suggested, hurriedly putting her skis back on. "It isn't that far away, and reindeer have amazing noses. She might even be able to tell that the ice is melting. We'd better be quick."

Despite the worry about the thaw,

Lotta couldn't help smiling as they made their way back through the forest. The sunlight was coming through the trees in bright shafts, and the place seemed to be suddenly alive with birds and tiny creatures.

Although the snow was softening underfoot, they could still easily see the tracks of the herd, so there was no danger of getting lost. Karl seemed to have perked up, even though he'd only had a quick feed, and he was dancing around Flower in circles. He reminded Lotta of a puppy, little and silly, with feet that were too big for him.

But as they came closer to the river, the girls grew quieter, listening for the sound of water. At last they came out through the trees to the riverbank, and stared in dismay at the sheet of ice they had walked over only three hours before.

It wasn't there any more. Now a jagged channel was running down the middle of the river – dark, fast-flowing water, dotted with huge chunks of ice. Lotta stepped up to the edge and peered over. The far bank seemed a lot further away than it had earlier on.

Erika kicked angrily at the snow with the point of her ski. "We can't cross here."

"Maybe there's a place further up. Somewhere we could just jump across the gap..." Lotta said, but her cousin shook her head.

"No, Lotta. Think! The meltwater is coming down from the mountains further up the river, isn't it? It'll be worse upstream. We'll have to find a place to cross downstream." Erika looked up and down the river, and Lotta gulped, trying to keep calm. She hadn't felt so out of place in this world since the first morning she'd found herself here. She just didn't know what to do.

"We won't know the way back..." she whispered.

"We'll find it somehow." Erika put an

arm round her shoulder. "Hey! Flower!"

The mother reindeer had been standing next to them, staring at the water, but now she turned and began to walk slowly but confidently away along the riverbank.

"Flower, come here!" Erika called, but Lotta caught her arm.

"Maybe we should follow her, Erika. She knows the way better than we do, doesn't she?"

The Sami herders didn't so much lead the reindeer as follow them, Lotta had realized during her time here. The reindeer knew where they were supposed to be going – it was more a case of keeping them all together, and protecting them on the way. The herd always returned to its traditional calving grounds and the same summer pastures. But sometimes they had to use different routes, depending on the weather.

"She seems to know where she's going," Lotta said, undoing her skis. Erika took hers off, too, and they began to follow Flower and Karl. "It's as if we've rescued her, and now she's going to help us."

They walked on down the riverbank, carrying their skis as they wove in and out of the trees, until Flower suddenly stopped. The river had widened out, and it didn't seem to be flowing quite as fast. The chunks of ice floated lazily by, and Lotta was sure she saw a fish dart past, too.

She thought that Flower had just stopped to drink, and the reindeer did lean down for a few mouthfuls of water. But then she stepped closer to the river,

and into the shallow water just below
the bank.

"She's going to cross!" Lotta gasped.
Even though the river seemed wider and
shallower here, now she came close it
still looked frightening. The water was
swirling by so fast, and she couldn't tell
how deep it was.

Flower went deeper into the water, so
that it was halfway up her legs, but Karl
and the girls didn't follow her. They stood
huddled on the bank, staring after her
miserably. The mother reindeer stopped,
realizing that her baby wasn't with her,
and turned round to eye them all. Lotta
was sure that if she could talk she would
have told them to hurry up and get on
with it. But then she stepped delicately
over to the bank and bumped Karl with

her nose, trying to encourage him into the water. The calf squealed, and jumped back. He'd never seen anything like the river before, and he didn't want to be in it.

"I think we have to go with her," Lotta said nervously. "She knows what she's doing. If she thinks it's safe for Karl, it should be safe for us, too."

"I suppose so..." Erika muttered. "Take off your boots and your coat. We'll bundle them up, and try and keep them out of the water. I can't tell how deep it is, but if we hold them up, we should be able to keep them dry."

Lotta nodded, shivering as she shrugged off her thick coat, and undid her boots. Her feet began to hurt as soon as she put them down in the snow. The water was going to be deathly cold.

Karl was still darting about on the bank, clearly anxious to reach his mother, but frightened of the rushing river.

Lotta looked at him. "Erika, can you take my things, and I'll carry Karl? He's never going to go in the water, is he?"

Erika nodded. "I'm not sure I am, either," she muttered, with a little shiver.

Lotta passed over her coat bundle and her skis, and picked Karl up. He struggled madly for a moment, but then Flower reached over and nipped at his ear with her teeth. Lotta thought she was probably telling him to behave. Flower stood in the water, just below the bank, looking from Lotta to Erika, as though she was making sure they were ready.

"Grab her antlers," Lotta said, looking at the swirling water. She tucked Karl tightly under her arm, and gripped on to Flower's antlers, grateful that she hadn't shed them yet.

With both girls holding on, Flower stepped forward into the water, and the girls followed, gasping as the cold hit them. The river was swollen with meltwater, and it was flowing so fast. Lotta felt herself being pushed hard against Flower's side by the strength of the rushing water. It was getting deeper and deeper, and as they reached the middle of the river it was up to Lotta's waist.

Karl wriggled and squealed as the cold water soaked his dangling legs, but thankfully he didn't try to leap away. Lotta wasn't sure she'd have been able to catch him.

Flower walked slowly, determinedly on, planting her strong hooves firmly on the riverbed, and hauling the girls with her, until at last they scrambled out on the other side. The reindeer then shook herself energetically all over them.

Lotta put Karl down gently. Her arms were aching from the effort of holding him so tightly against the pull of the river. Flower leaned down to nuzzle at her baby, and he snuggled against her.

"I wish I could just shake myself dry," Erika said, her teeth chattering violently as she tried to wring out the skirts of her *gakti*.

Lotta nodded. At least their reindeer-skin leggings had kept out almost all of the water. They were damp, but not soaked like the wool cloth of her tunic. She pushed her numb, icy feet into her boots, and gratefully dragged on her coat. Then both girls leaned against Flower, shaking with cold, and the fear that they'd had to hold back as they crossed the river.

CHAPTER NINE

"Can we sit and rest for a bit?" Erika murmured. She was shivering and pale, and Lotta hated the way her cheeks looked pinched with cold under her hat.

The two girls moved into the shelter of the trees, away from the rushing sound of the river and sat down, huddled together. Karl trotted over and nestled against Lotta's side, his head in her lap. Flower watched from a few paces away as the two girls slowly nibbled some of the dried meat they had brought with them. Then at last she came over to join them, lying down next to Erika, who leaned against her, grateful for her warmth.

A few hours later, Lotta woke up with a start, disturbed by a rustling in the trees. She sat up quickly, but it seemed to be only a red squirrel, peering down at her from the branches, his tufted ears twitching. Lotta took a deep breath, and then shifted uncomfortably in her damp *gakti*. She still felt cold, but better than before, less shaky and scared.

It was getting dark now – not very, but the light was starting to seep away, and the shadows of the trees were lengthening.

"Erika, wake up," Lotta said, reaching over and gently shaking her cousin. "We should go. It's late. We have to try and get back tonight. Mamma and Aunt Astri will be worried about us." Maybe they would have set out to find them, Lotta wondered, feeling guilty. The girls had held up the journey to the calving grounds. But Lotta still felt sure they couldn't have done anything else.

Erika sat up, yawning, but her cheeks

were pinkish again and she'd lost that awful chilled look. "Oh, we must have slept for ages." She struggled to her feet. "We have to go."

The girls strapped on their skis, and Flower nudged Karl to his feet. Then she set off through the trees again, with the girls walking on either side of her.

"Do you think she still knows where she's going?" Lotta asked.

Erika sighed. "I hope so…"

They trekked on, chilled and weary, until the light faded completely. Karl suddenly stopped, with a miserable little honk. He stood behind them, hooves planted in the snow in a determined sort of way.

"Come on, Karl," Erika called, trying to sound cheerful.

"I think he's saying he's not going any further," Lotta said. "Maybe we should camp out until morning. I know we walked in the dark last night, but then we had the trail to follow. If we go wrong now, we could get really lost."

We are really lost, a small voice inside her whispered, but she didn't say it out loud. "Look, we could camp over there." Not far away, a huge tree had fallen, and its roots made a patch of shelter, big enough for the two girls to curl up in and rest. Karl snuggled in with them, and Flower lay down outside, like a guard dog.

Lotta curled herself round Karl and Erika, and stared out at the dark forest. The moon wasn't as bright as it had been the night before, and everything seemed much more frightening. What if they never found their way back to the rest of the herd? Lotta was almost sure now that she was here because of Karl and Flower, to make sure that they got home safely. She had no idea how, or why. Or how she was going to get home herself. Surrounded as she was by darkness, and small, quiet noises, her everyday life seemed very far away.

"Lotta… It's morning."

Lotta rolled over, rubbing at her damp face, and Karl jumped away with a startled squeak.

Erika giggled. "He was licking your cheek. I let him, I thought it might be a nice way to wake up."

"Uurgh!" Lotta groaned, as she scrambled to her feet. "I'm cold right through. I don't think I've properly got warm since the river."

"Hopefully you'll warm up when we're walking. We have to go, look. Flower's set off already."

Flower was several paces away, loudly grunting to Karl to follow her. She looked over at Erika and Lotta, as if to tell them that they'd better hurry up, too.

"We'll get back to the rest of the herd today," Lotta said, as they set off on their skis. She was trying to sound sure.

"I really hope so," Erika said. "They must be so worried about us, my mamma and yours. Especially now we've been away overnight. And they can't go on to the calving ground until they've found us. They'll have gone to look for us, but it won't be easy to find our tracks, not with the way the herd churn up the snow."

"I suppose I shouldn't have made us go," Lotta said in a small voice.

But Erika shook her head. "No. We had to. And anyway, you didn't make me. We couldn't have left Flower behind."

Lotta smiled at her gratefully, and then she gasped. "Erika, look!"

They were joining a wider path between the trees, and Flower was looking out along it, as if she was considering the way. Then she bent her head down, snuffling confidently, as though she'd caught a scent she knew. The girls hurried after her, and stared at the path – at the churned-up snow, covered in hoofprints, and marked here and there by the thick wooden runners of the sledges.

"We found them! The trail!" Lotta and Erika hugged each other excitedly.

"All we have to do now is follow it, and we'll find them!" Erika squealed.

"I wonder how far we've got to go," Lotta said, peering around at the trees. "I don't remember this part of the forest. It must be a bit we went through when I was asleep on the sledge."

"Lotta, hush a moment." Erika caught her arm, her fingers pinching, and Lotta stopped talking, suddenly frightened.

"I heard something – oh, there it is again!" Erika's eyes widened with fear as the noise floated out across the forest, and Lotta let out a terrified gasp. She had never heard that sound before, not for real. But she knew at once what it was.

The howl of a wolf...

"Can you see them?" Erika asked, looking frantically from side to side.

"Them?" Lotta faltered.

"They always hunt in packs," Erika told her grimly. "They'll be after Karl – he's the smallest and weakest. Easy prey."

Flower seemed to know this, too. She had nudged Karl close in to her side, and her head was lowered, ready to use her antlers to protect her baby.

Lotta pulled out her knife, but she knew they would never be able to fight off a whole pack of wolves, or even a small hunting group. "Look, if we keep going, we might get back to the herd before they're brave enough to attack us."

Erika nodded, getting her knife out, too. "It's our only chance. Come on, Flower." She grabbed Flower's antlers, and the girls pulled her forward, hurrying along the trail. Karl scurried beside them, quiet and frightened. He had never seen wolves, either, but he must have been able to smell that they were dangerous.

"I can see one," Lotta gasped, a few minutes later. "Over there, look."

A thin, dog-like shape was slinking through the trees alongside them. It was whiter than Lotta had expected, and the sun shone on its fur. If she hadn't been running away from it, she would have thought it was beautiful. Instead, it was the most frightening thing she had ever seen.

She strode along on her skis, trying desperately to go faster, but the wolf kept pace with them easily, drawing closer between the trees. Soon Lotta could see two more of the pack at its heels.

"They're on this side, too," Erika told her, panting. "Oh! Look out!" She shoved Lotta to the side as one of the wolves darted in, trying to snap at Flower.

The reindeer let out a snarling grunt, and lowered her antlers, charging at the wolf, who rolled quickly out of the way. But there were five or six of them now – Lotta couldn't be quite sure, they were so fast. And they dashed in, one after the other, snapping at Flower's legs and even leaping for her neck.

Lotta seized Karl, holding him close, and stretching out her shaking hand with the knife. She had no idea how to use it, even, but perhaps the wolves had seen hunters before. They seemed to be wary of the girls and their weapons. For the moment, anyway.

Four wolves were circling Flower now, darting in and out, snapping here and there as she turned, grunting and charging at them, antlers down. Then all at once they rushed forward, two of them leaping for her back at the same time. One of them tore a scratch down Flower's shoulder, and she screamed and galloped away, vanishing between the trees.

"Flower!" Lotta called. But she was gone.

Karl let out a despairing little whinny as his mother disappeared, and Lotta sobbed with fear. Two of the wolves were still left, circling widely around the two girls and the little reindeer. Clearly they thought that Karl would be easier pickings than his mother.

"Stand back to back!" Erika gasped, holding out her knife, and Lotta nodded, pressing her back against her cousin's, Karl trembling in her arms. She couldn't let the wolves have the calf. Not after they had tried so hard to keep him alive. It was why she was here!

There were more wolves now – the whole pack was back again, creeping closer and closer.

"I think Flower outran them…" Erika muttered. "They've come back for Karl. And us, maybe. If they're really hungry."

What would happen if I was eaten by a wolf in a dream? Lotta wondered. If it wasn't a dream, she didn't even want to think about it. She gritted her teeth, and tried to stare back at the circling wolves. She mustn't look afraid.

"Lotta! Lotta, look!" Erika was screaming, and Lotta whirled round in a panic, wondering if the wolf had jumped at her cousin. But instead the wolves were retreating. Slowly, reluctantly, they were slinking back into the trees. Lotta could hear them growling and barking furiously.

She shook her head, not understanding why they were giving up – but then she realized that it wasn't the wolves she could hear at all.

It was shouting, angry shouting, and the thudding of hooves. A sledge was racing through the trees towards them, drawn by two heavy reindeer and driven by her cousin Johan. Beside it ran Matti, gripping the antlers of another reindeer – one still with both her antlers, and a bleeding cut down her shoulder.

CHAPTER TEN

"How did you find us?" Lotta gasped, hugging Johan.

"Flower showed us the way." He smiled down at them both. "She must have smelled these two that we've got pulling the sledge, she ran straight towards us. Matti tried to catch her, but she kept darting away."

"Then we realized she wanted us to come after her," Matti explained. "She kept stopping and looking back, to make sure we were following. Then we heard you shouting at the wolves, but they fled when they saw us coming."

"Oh, Flower!" Lotta patted her lovingly. "And we thought you just ran off."

Erika shuddered. "Please can we get away from here? That was the most frightening thing that's ever happened to me."

"Yes, come on, let's get back to the rest of the herd. It isn't that far." Johan packed the girls on to the big sledge, tucking furs around them. He put Karl on Lotta's lap. "Everyone is going to be so glad to see you," he added. "We've all been out searching for you – I don't think Aunt Inge or Aunt Astri slept at all last night. You had them so worried."

"Sorry..." Lotta whispered, wrapping her arms tightly round Karl.

Johan turned his reindeer around, and Matti walked beside the sledge, leading Flower. She kept looking over and sniffing at Karl, as if she was making sure he was still there.

It wasn't long before the girls heard the

sounds of the other reindeer, the clonging of the bells and their grunting.

"We've got them!" Johan was calling, as they swept into the camp. "Aunt Inge! Aunt Astri! We found the girls!"

Lotta didn't even have time to get off the sledge before her mamma had come running, and swept her up into her arms.

"Oh, Lotta, oh, Lotta, I didn't think we'd ever see you again." Mamma was crying, and Lotta felt awful.

"I'm so sorry, I'm so sorry," she kept muttering into Mamma's neck. "We shouldn't have gone, but I hated leaving Flower behind. I thought Karl would die."

"I know – we should have sent you and the older boys back together to find her," Mamma said, holding Lotta out to look at her, as though to check she was all in one piece. "You're true reindeer girls, both of you. You were thinking of the reindeer before yourselves. But the danger! What if there had been a bear?" Then she caught sight of Flower, pressed close up against Lotta and Erika, with Karl snuggled in next to her. "She's been hurt! Oh, Lotta! What happened?"

"There were wolves," Lotta whispered, burying her face in her mamma's coat again. "Flower led the boys to us just in time to scare them away. We saved her, but then she saved us twice, Mamma. She led us back over the river, and we'd never have been able to cross it without her. And then the wolves…"

"She's amazing," Erika agreed. "We wouldn't have got back without her. And she protected her baby the whole time. She drew the wolves away from him."

"You girls should have them," Johan suggested. "Erika's oldest, so she should have Flower, and Lotta should have Karl. You're both old enough to have your own reindeer."

Lotta let out a little gasp, turning to look up hopefully at her mamma. If they were to be given their own reindeer, a tiny change would be made to the family earmark to show that the deer were theirs.

"Yes." Her mamma nodded, glancing at Aunt Astri. "But only if you promise you will never, ever go off like that again."

"I promise!" Lotta hugged her mamma tightly. "Thank you!"

"Wolves! Real wolves?" little Nils asked, his eyes glowing with excitement in the firelight. "I wish I'd been there."

Lotta shuddered. "Yes, real wolves. And you wouldn't have liked it, Nils. It was horrible. They were frightening!"

They were sitting round the fire, wrapped up in reindeer furs, drinking hot soup that Aunt Astri had made.

It was strange, Lotta thought – Mamma and Aunt Astri and the others were half cross with her and Erika, and half proud of them for rescuing Flower and Karl.

Johan pushed through the doorway to the *lavvu* just then, and nodded. "Exactly. Very frightening. Don't you ever think of doing anything like that, Nils. But Lotta, Erika, see what I've just found. I went out to check on Flower and Karl, and put some more ointment on that cut on her shoulder, and look." He brought his hand round from behind his back and held something out.

"She shed her antlers!" Lotta said, nearly spilling the soup in her excitement. "Oh, I'm glad she still had them when she had to fight off the wolves."

"Mmm-hmm, she was lucky," Johan

agreed, sitting down by the fire, and
pulling out his knife.

"What are you
going to carve?"
Erika asked,
as he began to
scrape away at
the reindeer horn
with the blade.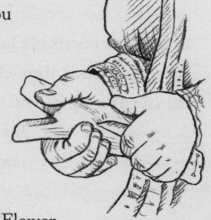

Johan smiled. "Flower.
So we remember your journey with her."

"We wouldn't forget," Erika said with
a shiver. "Those wolves…"

Lotta wriggled closer to her cousin, and
wrapped an arm round her. "It was a real
adventure, wasn't it? And we did save
Flower and Karl."

Erika smiled and hugged Lotta back.
"Yes, we did…"

The two girls leaned against each other, and gazed into the firelight. Lotta watched the flames leap and twist, and she seemed to see the reindeer galloping through them. Now the wolves, twisting and turning in their terrifying dance. Then the flames died down a little, and there were only the trees, the branches swaying in the wind. And one reindeer, grazing quietly beneath them, a tiny calf close to her side.

"Goodnight, Flower," Lotta whispered. "Goodbye, Karl…"

"What did you say, Lotta?"

Lotta blinked, looking up at Erika. But Erika had changed…

Oldeforeldre was smiling down at her. Lotta had blankets wrapped round her instead of furs, and she was leaning against Oldeforeldre's chair. The door to the rest of the house was open, and she could hear a quiet buzz of chatter. The party seemed to be winding down – most of the guests must have gone.

"Lotta?" Her mum looked round the door. "Oh, you're here. You need to go upstairs to bed soon, it's ever so late. Say goodnight to Oldeforeldre. I'll be back in a bit."

Lotta nodded, and looked round at Oldeforeldre. "Was I asleep for a long time? I had the strangest dream..." She smiled up at her great-grandmother. "You were in it... I think it was the best dream I've ever had." She rubbed her hand across her eyes, trying to remember properly. Dreams slipped away, and she didn't ever want to forget this one. "We'd saved Flower and Karl, and Johan and Mamma and Aunt Astri said that we could have them for our own, me and you. Karl was going to be mine."

Oldeforeldre's face changed. Her eyes widened in shock, and she leaned down to Lotta. "What did you say? Flower? You saved Flower? And the baby? Karl?"

"Mmm. And there were wolves," Lotta added sleepily. "Johan and Matti chased them away."

"Lotta, I never told you this..." Oldeforeldre looked confused, but excited, too. "You couldn't have known about Flower. I don't think I've ever told anyone about her, not even your mormor. It was so sad. I wanted to forget, but I never have."

Lotta looked up at her, her eyes full of tears. "Then – when that was all real – could you not save Flower?"

Oldeforeldre looked down at her hands, twisting them over and over. "Flower came back – she managed to find us all in the end. But by then, her calf… He was so little and he wouldn't take any food, even though we tried so hard, my cousin Lotta and I. He died, Lotta."

"He didn't." Lotta shook her head firmly. "We went and got Flower. We brought her back for him."

Oldeforeldre laughed, but she was crying at the same time. "I almost believe you did," she murmured. Then she got up carefully, balancing on her stick. "Stay there, Lotta. I have something for you." She went over to a wooden box in the corner of the room and lifted the lid, searching around inside it.

Lotta leaned against the chair, wrapped in her blankets.

She looked up as Oldeforeldre came back, carrying something small, wrapped in a piece of blue cloth. Lotta was almost sure it was part of a *gakti*. She could see the embroidery.

"Here." Oldeforeldre pressed it into

her hands. She was smiling, but Lotta could see the shining tracks of tears on her cheeks.

Lotta unwrapped the little bundle and laughed delightedly as she held up a tiny piece of carved reindeer horn. "Johan's carving! He finished it!"

Her great-grandmother nodded. "Yes. It took him all that springtime, until we reached the summer pastures. Weeks of work."

"It's beautiful," Lotta whispered, standing up to hold the carving closer to the light. "And so delicate. She even has her earmarks, I can feel them! I can't believe he managed to carve Karl, too, when he was so tiny."

"What?" Oldeforeldre peered over at the carving. "No, Lotta. It's only Flower.

Johan carved it for me and my cousin Lotta, I remember." She sighed. "He didn't put Karl in, after what happened. It was too sad."

Lotta shook her head and smiled, turning the little carving around. "But he did. Look."

She held the carving out to show her great-grandmother – a mother reindeer, her head curved lovingly round her baby, walking safe by her side.

GLOSSARY

Beaska – a thick coat made from reindeer fur

Bunad – a traditional folk costume in Norway, often worn by the Sami. Nowadays people wear them for special occasions

Four Winds Cap – a Sami hat with four points, which represent the winds from the north, south, east and west

Gákti – a Sami tunic that is often finely embroidered and decorated with buttons and jewellery

Joik – a Sami song, often sung without instruments

Lavvu – a Sami tent, supported by wooden poles and traditionally covered with reindeer hides

Lutefisk – a smelly fish dish, made from whitefish that has been soaked to give it a jelly-like texture

Morfar – Grandfather

Mormor – Grandmother

Nisse – a Norwegian elf. Nisse may be small but they are very strong. They protect farmers and their children at night

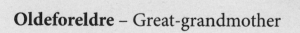

Oldeforeldre – Great-grandmother

Pepperkaken – Christmas biscuits made with ginger and other spices

A REINDEER'S LIFE

Reindeer live in the far north of Europe, Russia and America, in a region known as the Arctic. These animals are very tough, with thick coats to keep out the freezing cold. Even baby reindeer are sturdy – at just one day old, a calf can outrun a grown man!

Reindeer are the only kind of deer where both males and females grow antlers. The males use their antlers for fighting over mates, whilst the females use them to protect their babies. The deer lose their antlers by the spring – the females keep theirs for a little longer than the males. Both have to regrow them by the autumn. Antlers grow amazingly quickly – up to 2.5 cm in a day! And just like human fingerprints, no two sets of antlers are the same.

Reindeer eat moss and grass, but their favourite food is lichen, which is what brings them to their winter feeding grounds in the mountains. They use their antlers and hooves to clear snow to get to their food.

LOOKING AFTER REINDEER

For hundreds of years, the Sami people have helped guide reindeer to their different pastures throughout the seasons. They have a special relationship with the deer, keeping an eye out for danger – such as wolves and bears – and making sure they don't fall off cliffs or get lost. The Sami can even find the best snow for the deer to dig beneath for lichen. In return, the deer provide them with meat, hides and antlers, and before the Sami had snowmobiles, the deer pulled their sledges too.

The herds are semi-wild, allowed to roam freely during the summer months and deciding when it is time to migrate. But the Sami know their deer well – they have over 200 words to describe them! Each family group also has a special mark that they cut into their deers' ears to tell them apart from other herds.

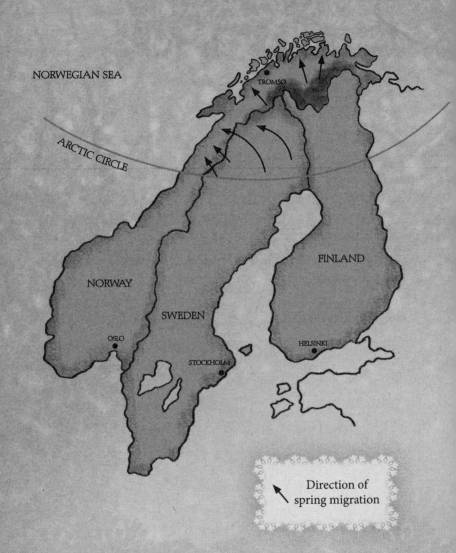

SAMI MIGRATION

NORWEGIAN SEA

ARCTIC CIRCLE

TROMSØ

FINLAND

NORWAY

SWEDEN

OSLO

STOCKHOLM

HELSINKI

Direction of
spring migration

Seasons and hours of daylight

Winter	Spring	Summer	Autumn	Winter

| Jan | Feb | Mar | Apr | May | Jun | Jul | Aug | Sep | Oct | Nov |

THROUGH
THE SEASONS

In the winter the reindeer look for food in the highlands of Norway, Sweden and Finland.

When spring comes, the Sami men take the pregnant females to the lowlands on a long, safe route. The migration must be timed so it's light enough to travel, as winter in the Arctic Circle means full days of darkness. Later, the rest of the Sami family herd the males on a shorter but more difficult route towards the coast to feed.

The females give birth to their calves in the lowlands, and then join up with the males again. Some Sami families will even herd their deer out to the islands – the calves are strong enough to swim in the sea by the summer. The summer months have very long days, with a "midnight sun" that rises in May and doesn't fully set until July.

Then, in the autumn, the Sami turn their herds back towards the highlands, ready to start a new winter.

TOP DOGS

The Finnish Lapphund
has been specially bred
to herd reindeer.

The dogs bark
to one another to
help the pack direct
the deer.

These dogs
have an excellent
sense of smell and
hearing for tracking
down lost deer.

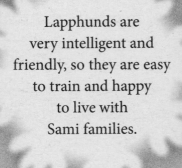

Lapphunds are
very intelligent and
friendly, so they are easy
to train and happy
to live with
Sami families.

Their thick,
warm coats come in
lots of different colours,
often with "spectacles"
markings!

AWAY FROM HOME

By the nineteenth century, life began to change for the Sami. The Norwegian government decided that Sami children should learn Norwegian instead of their own language. Once the children reached about seven years old, they had to leave their families and go to boarding school. They were only allowed to go home at Christmas and during the summer holidays.

For many children, this was a difficult time. They missed their old lives and began to forget their own language. Nowadays, very few people can speak Sami fluently, although many are still proud of their history and keep up the old way of life.

THE SNOW BEAR

FROM BEST-SELLING AUTHOR
HOLLY WEBB

A beautiful Christmas story,
perfect for bedtime reading

As the snow begins to fall
just days before Christmas,
Grandad helps Sara build an
igloo in the garden with a small
snow bear to watch over it.

And when Sara wakes in the
middle of the night, it looks
very different outside. She sets out
on an enchanted journey through
a world of ice, but will she ever
find her way home…

HOLLY WEBB

Holly Webb started out as a children's book editor, and wrote her first series for the publisher she worked for. She has been writing ever since, with over seventy books to her name. Holly lives in Berkshire, with her husband and three young sons. She has two pet cats, called Milly and Marble, who are always nosying around when Holly is trying to type on her laptop.

For more information about Holly Webb visit:

www.holly-webb.com